Benny
and the Important Job

Roley
and the Woodland Walk

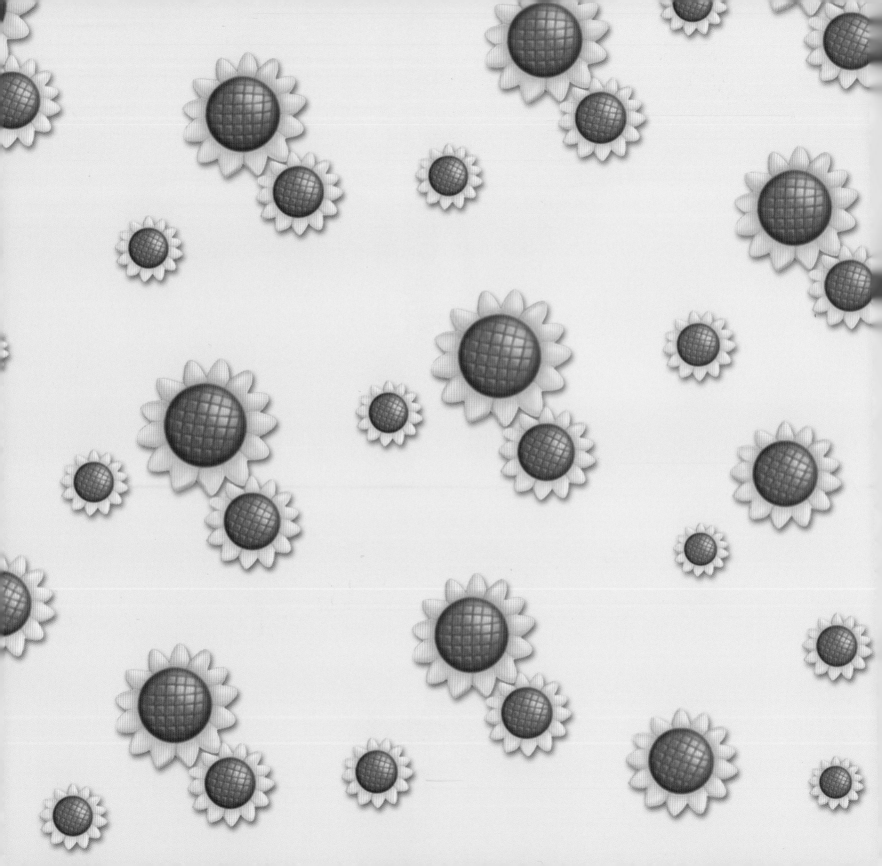

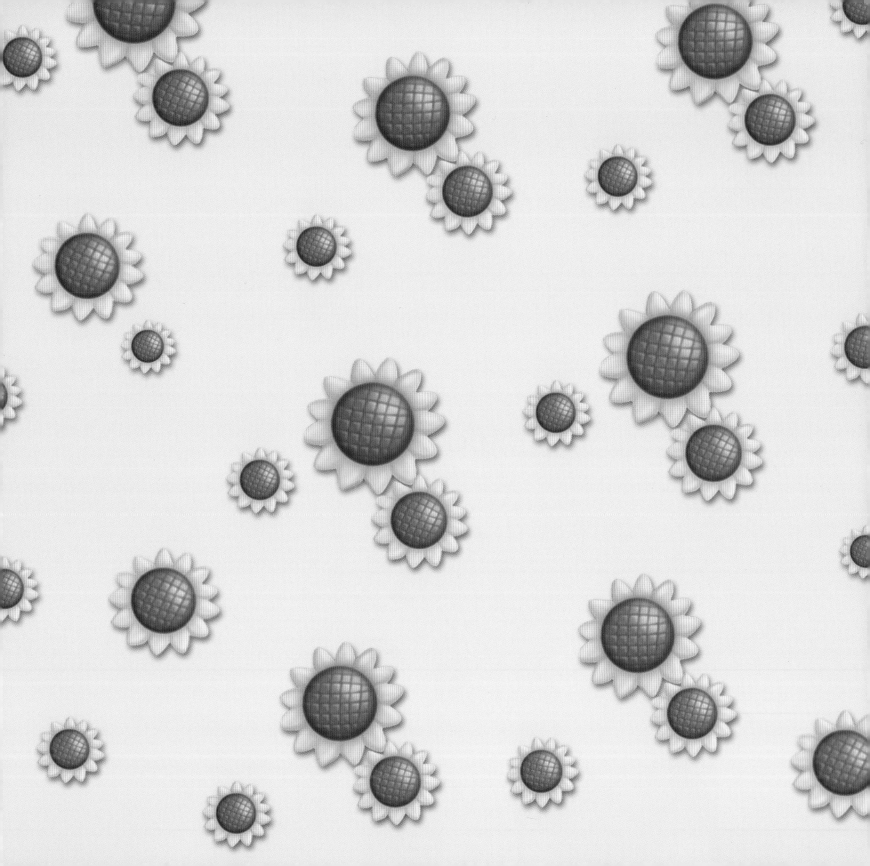

EGMONT

We bring stories to life

This edition published for BCA in 2008
First published in Great Britain 2008
by Egmont UK Limited,
239 Kensington High Street, London W8 6SA

HiT entertainment

ISBN 978 0 6035 6380 5

1 3 5 7 9 10 8 6 4 2
Printed in Italy

Contents

Benny
and the Important Job

Roley
and the Woodland Walk

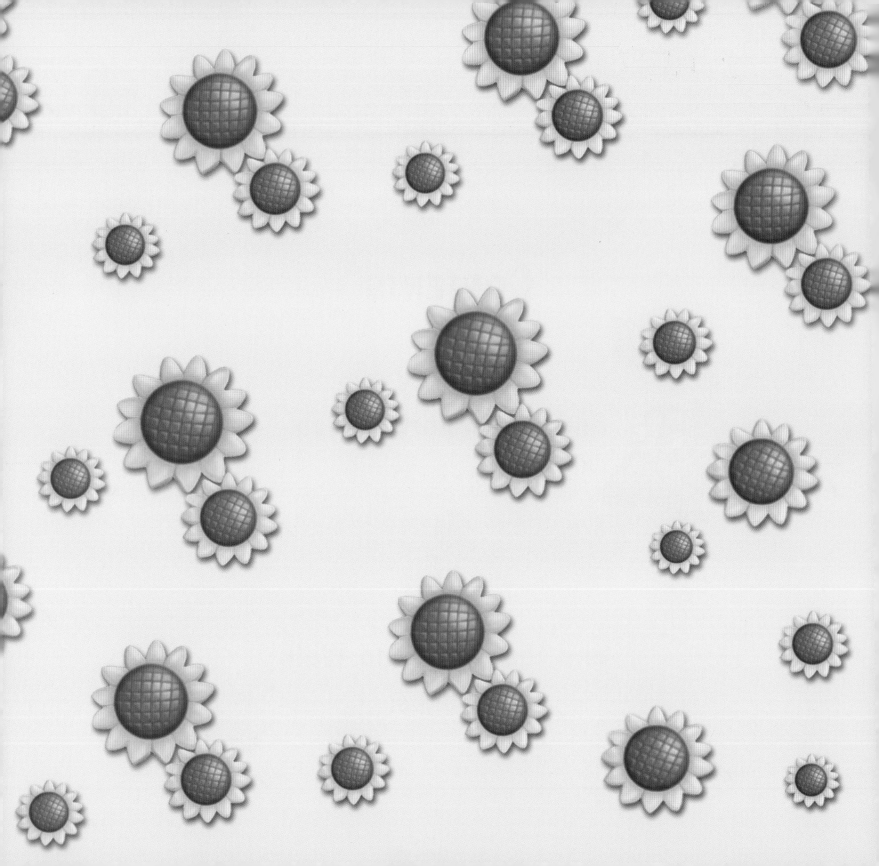

Benny
and the Important Job

Illustrations by Dynamo and Jerry Smith

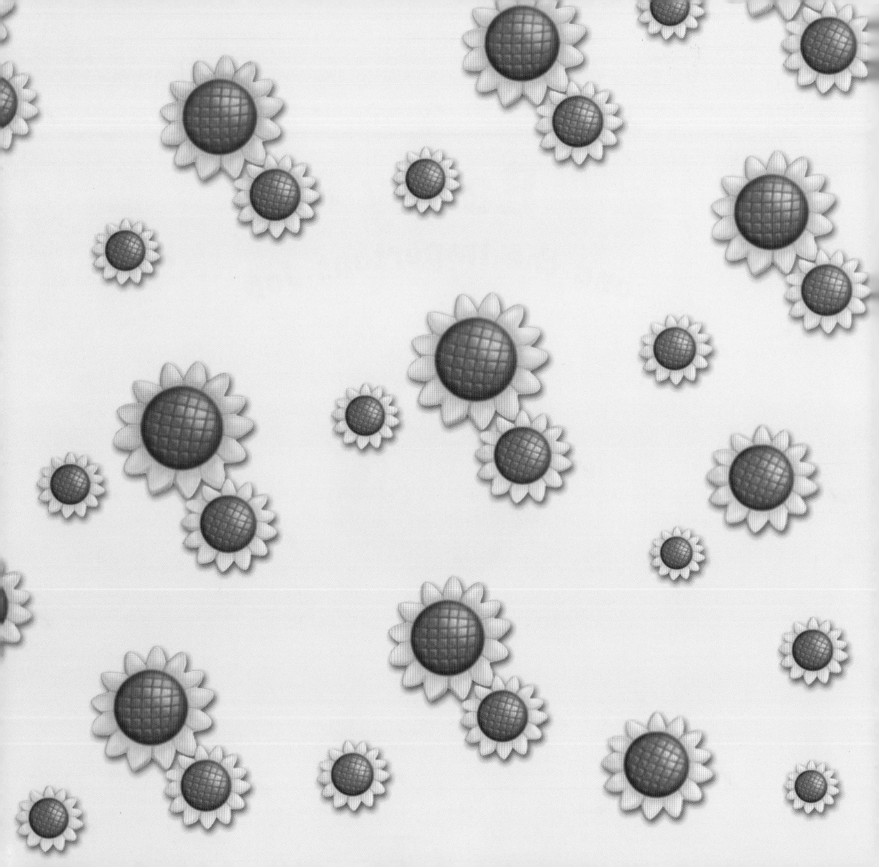

Bob and the machines are busy with a big job – they are building a special house for the Bentleys. Benny wants to help, but is the job too big for him?

Early one morning, Benny the little digger zoomed into Sunflower Valley. The machines were all still fast asleep in their shelter.

"Hey, everyone! Wake up!" said Benny.

Bob came to the door of his caravan. "What's going on?" he yawned.

"There was no work for me in Bobsville today, so I've come to help!" said Benny.

"OK, team, rise and shine!" said Bob.

Soon, Benny was following Bob and the team to the site. He was very excited.

"We're building a special house for the Bentleys today," said Bob, "*inside* this hill!"

"Unreal!" smiled Benny.

"That's just brilliant!" giggled Dizzy.

"Who would have thought!" smiled Scoop.

Mr Bentley arrived to help, too.

"Let's start! What am I doing first?" said Benny, excitedly.

"We need to mark out the foundations. Then Scoop and Muck can start digging," Bob told the machines.

"No prob, Bob!" said Scoop.

"Let's get mucky!" added Muck.

Benny wondered what his job would be.

"When the foundations are ready, Roley can level the ground," said Bob.

"Rock and roll!" revved Roley.

"And Dizzy and I will make concrete blocks for the walls," said Bob.

"I know the perfect place to make them," said Dizzy.

Bob and Dizzy rushed away, leaving Benny behind with Mr Bentley.

Benny wanted to help Scoop and Muck, but Mr Bentley was worried. "This is really a job for big diggers, Benny," he said.

"Little diggers can dig big holes too, you know!" said Benny, crossly.

"OK, but it must be ready tomorrow," said Mr Bentley. "A photographer is coming — our house is going to be on the cover of a magazine!"

Benny began to dig, but the ground was so hard that his digger bounced right off!

"Everything needs to be ready for tomorrow, remember!" said Mr Bentley.

Muck and Scoop had finished digging their holes, so they helped Benny with his.

Benny was sad. "That was my big, important job," he sighed.

The next morning, Bob and the machines reached the site.

Lofty and Wendy brought big glass windows for the Bentleys' house.

"Well done, Wendy," said Mr Bentley. "And well done, Lofty, too!"

"The windows are here, the hill's dug . . . now to mix the concrete," said Bob.

"I'll do it!" said Benny.

"Ha, ha! Don't be silly!" laughed Dizzy.
"How can a digger mix concrete?"

"Oh," sighed Benny. He looked sad.

There were lots of jobs for the machines to do,
but poor Benny was too small or too slow for
any of them.

Muck and Scoop went to fetch the concrete blocks.

Roley rolled the ground flat.

Bob fixed a waterproof sheet to the roof of the new hill house.

And Wendy and Lofty fitted the windows.

Benny watched them, miserably. "Nobody needs a little digger like me. I'll just go back to Bobsville," he cried.

But just then, Mrs Bentley and Scrambler arrived. His trailer was loaded with plants.

"Wicked house!" smiled Scrambler.

"Now we just need to put these plants in the garden," said Mrs Bentley.

Mr Bentley gasped. "The photographer from the magazine is coming any minute!"

"What are we going to do?" cried Mrs Bentley. "There's so much digging to do!"

Muck and Scoop wanted to help, but they were too big and heavy to dig the ground.

"I'm small enough," said Benny. "It can be my big, important job!"

"Come on then, Benny! Let's get planting!" smiled Mrs Bentley.

Benny had just finished digging when the photographer, David Daley, arrived. "What a gorgeous home!" he said.

"It's all down to Bob's crew… especially Benny the digger!" smiled Mr Bentley.

"Let's have a picture," said David Daley. "Join in, Benny. Now smile, everyone!"

The biggest smile belonged to Benny, the little digger.

THE END

Roley
and the Woodland Walk

Illustrations by Craig Cameron

When Roley tries to help his woodland friends, they get in the way of Bob and Wendy's work. Until Roley comes up with a brilliant idea . . .

It was a very hot day in Sunflower Valley.

Bob and Wendy were on their way to build workbenches and fit big tools in the workshop.

"We don't need any help, today," said Bob. "So you can all have the day off!"

The machines wanted to keep cool in the shade. So off they all went to the shelter to play 'I Spy'. Except for Roley . . .

Roley set off into Sunflower Valley to look for his friend, Birdie.

"Birdie," called Roley. "It's your friend, Roley. Birdie! Where are you?"

Roley came to a pond in the clearing, but the hot weather had dried up all the water. Next to the pond, he saw Birdie, looking sad. Roley didn't know what was wrong.

"You're not whistling," worried Roley. "Are you too hot?"

Birdie chirped weakly. Roley wondered how he could help. "Maybe I could find you somewhere to keep cool?"

Just then, Birdie's chicks flew on to Roley's cab. As Roley set off to find some shade, a squirrel hopped out of the trees. He was hot, too. "Don't worry," said Roley, kindly.

"I'll come back for you."

Roley gave Birdie and her chicks a ride to the storeroom. When they arrived, they flew off his cab and headed for the workshop.

"No, no! Not in there. That's where Bob and Wendy are working," he said, and guided them into the cool storeroom.

Then Roley set off to fetch the squirrel.

Wendy and Bob were building a new cupboard to keep all the tools tidy.

They went to the storeroom to get the first big tool – the saw.

They didn't see Birdie and her chicks nestling under the cover!

Roley zoomed back to the clearing. "It's all right, little squirrel," said Roley. "I've got a lovely place for you out of the sun."

Suddenly, three more squirrels scampered down the trees. "Climb aboard," smiled Roley. Just as he was about to leave, a family of otters dashed out of the bushes. They were hot and thirsty, too.

"Stay here. I'll be right back!" said Roley.

Roley dropped the squirrels off at the storeroom, and then went to fetch the otters.

With the tool cupboard finished, Wendy and Bob wanted to fit the big saw. But when Wendy found the instructions, they were full of holes!

"Oh, no! We can't read this," said Wendy. "Something's been pecking at them!"

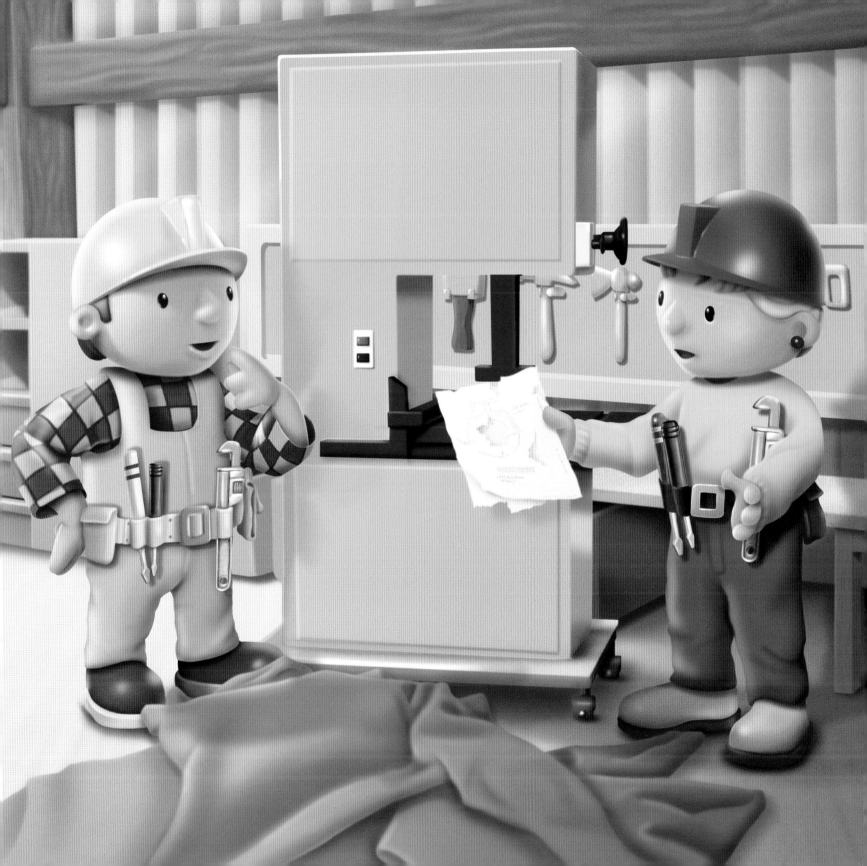

Bob and Wendy couldn't fit the saw without the instructions. They decided to fit the next big tool instead – the drill.

As Wendy pulled off the cover, the squirrels scurried away to hide.

"Look, Wendy!" cried Bob. "These instructions are torn, too."

They were really puzzled now!

Roley brought the otters to the storeroom and looked around inside. "Little squirrel . . . Birdie?" he called. "Are you still in there?"

But they weren't! All the animals were in the workshop.

Roley didn't want Bob to see the animals, so he thought of a plan. "I found Birdie. Um . . . she's not well. She needs our help!" he said, making it up.

Roley took Bob to the dried-up pond.

"Birdie must be thirsty!" said Bob. "When ponds dry up, birds and animals can't get any water. The best way to help is to put some out for them." Then Bob poured water from his flask. "Now when Birdie comes back, she can have a drink."

Then, Bob and Roley rolled back to the workshop.

Back at the workshop, Wendy had some news for them. "Bob!" she called. "I know why everything was chewed and pecked! The workshop was full of animals! I gave them some water and they've all gone away happy."

Roley felt bad, so he told Bob what had happened. "Don't worry, Roley," said Bob. You were only trying to help."

Suddenly, Roley had a brilliant idea . . .

Roley asked the other machines to help gather up old bits of wood so Bob and Wendy could build a bird table. That way, his woodland friends would have food and water, and he would see them all the time.

The team worked together and soon the bird table was finished. "Rock and roll!" smiled Roley.

And now, whenever the animals get thirsty or hot, they visit Roley's bird table.

THE END

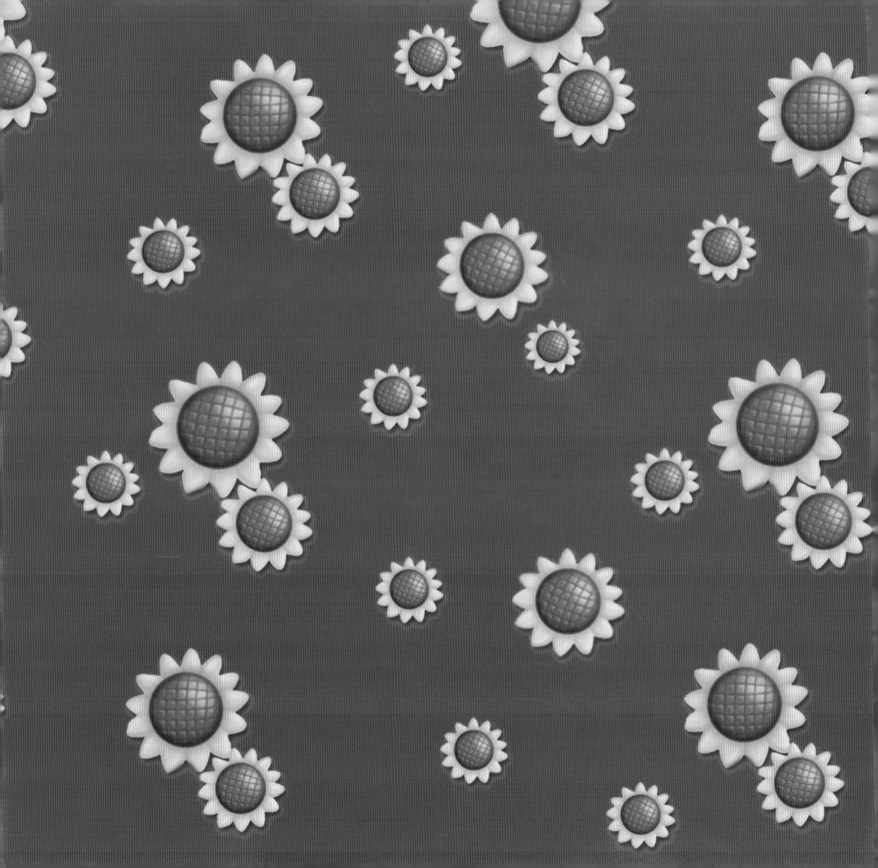

Two fun stories from the
Bob the Builder Story Library:

Benny and the Important Job
Roley and the Woodland Walk

Other titles in the series

HiT entertainment

egmont.co.uk

ISBN 978-0-6035-6380-5

9 780603 563805

www.bobthebuilder.com